J.P. and the POLKA-DOTTED ALIENS

ANA CRESPO

Pictures by
ERICA SIROTICH

Albert Whitman & Company
Chicago, Illinois

To Pedro.
Thank you for always supporting my dreams.
Love you!—AC

For Kevin,
who believes in me always—ES

Library of Congress Cataloging-in-Publication
data is on file with the publisher.

Text copyright © 2015 by Ana Crespo
Pictures copyright © 2015 by Albert Whitman & Company
Pictures by Erica Sirotich
Published in 2015 by Albert Whitman & Company
ISBN 978-0-8075-3977-4

Printed in China
10 9 8 7 6 5 4 3 2 1 HH 20 19 18 17 16 15

Design by Jordan Kost

For more information about Albert Whitman & Company,
visit our web site at www.albertwhitman.com.

I am JP the monkey.

I am playful. I am silly.

I am fun.

But sometimes I don't feel like a fun monkey.

Sometimes I feel mad.

Like when the polka-dotted aliens
invaded my spaceship.

The polka-dotted aliens

came in through secret tunnels.

They attacked my spaceship

and decorated it.

I almost screamed.
I was so mad.

Then I remembered I am a fun monkey.

I made some funny monkey faces.

I did a monkey dance.

I made some
silly monkey
sounds.

The polka-dotted aliens laughed.

I laughed too.

We had a fancy outer-space tea party.

It was a blast.

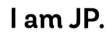

I am JP.

I am playful.

I am silly.

I am fun.

Sometimes I feel mad...

but having fun feels
a lot better.

A Note to Parents and Teachers from the Author

Everyone feels mad sometimes. Most adults know how to channel their anger. However, children do not always know how to express that emotion and that can lead to temper tantrums. Frustration with younger siblings, hunger, or tiredness can all contribute to a child feeling angry.

When I was younger, I didn't understand the ways children act out when experiencing anger. If I saw a child crying at the supermarket, I was annoyed and blamed the parents for not "handling" the situation. Once I became a parent, the crying didn't bother me so much. Just a few years ago, I was the parent with a crying child at the supermarket, wishing I could shape-shift into an ostrich and bury my face in the sand. But there are other ways to deal with temper tantrums—and superpowers, although useful, are not required.

Here are a few things you can do if your child is having a temper tantrum:

Stay calm no matter how difficult. **Distract** (or redirect) the child with games or toys or even silly faces. (In our story, JP finds comfort in pretending to be a monkey, making noises, and dancing.) **Remove the child** from the environment and place him on a quick time-out. Depending on the child's age, two to five minutes should be appropriate. **Set clear limits and expectations.** For example, while it is okay to feel mad or angry, it's not okay to hit people. **Encourage the use of words** to express feelings and to find out what exactly is causing the outburst. **Teach empathy** by helping the child see how his behavior affects others. **Do not shame** the child for expressing his feelings, even if those feelings could have been expressed in a more appropriate manner.

Here are a few everyday ways that may help your child avoid angry outbursts:

Maintain open communication with the child. If the child feels insecure expressing her feelings, she may avoid sharing with you again. **Praise and reward** the child appropriately. If the child receives attention only when behaving badly, she will continue to repeat the bad behavior.

Temper tantrums are relatively common between the ages of eighteen months and four years old and are perfectly natural. However, in certain circumstances, temper tantrums may be caused by more serious family problems. Talk to your doctor if you feel your child's behavior needs special attention.

Above all, listen to what your child's emotions are saying. Our children speak to us in ways that are not always direct because they don't have the words to describe what they're experiencing. Listening to children's emotions helps parents and caregivers raise happy, healthy adults.

Please note that I am not a specialist in the field of children's emotions. My experience and knowledge come from being a parent and conducting my own research. For additional information specific to your needs, please seek a professional opinion.

References:

American Academy of Pediatrics. "Temper tantrums: a normal part of growing up." *Pediatric Patient Education*. 2009. http://patientid.aap.org/content2.aspx?aid=5725.

Fetsch, R. J., and B. Jacobson. "Children's Anger and Tantrums." *Colorado State University Extension*. August 5, 2014. http://www.ext.colostate.edu/pubs/consumer/10248.html.

Kaneshiro, Neil K. "Temper tantrums." *MedlinePlus*. May 10, 2013. http://www.nlm.nih.gov/medlineplus/ency/article/001922.htm.

Mayo Clinic Staff. "Temper tantrums in toddlers: How to keep the peace." *Mayo Clinic*. August 10, 2012. http://www.mayoclinic.org/healthy-living/infant-and-toddler-health/in-depth/tantrum/art-20047845?pg=1.